Stand Up for Respect

Growing Character

By Frank Murphy

21st Century Junior Library

Published in the United States of America by
Cherry Lake Publishing
Ann Arbor, Michigan
www.cherrylakepublishing.com

Reading Adviser: Marla Conn, MS, Ed., Literacy specialist, Read-Ability, Inc.

Photo Credits: ©Monkey Business Images/Shutterstock, cover, 1; ©wavebreakmedia/Shutterstock, 4; ©ESB Professional/Shutterstock, 6; ©Rawpixel.com/Shutterstock, 8; ©Artazum/Shutterstock, 10; ©fizkes/Shutterstock, 12; ©Rido/Shutterstock, 14; ©Tyler Olson/Shutterstock, 16; ©Hurst Photo/Shutterstock, 18; ©Monkey Business Images/Shutterstock, 20

Library of Congress Cataloging-in-Publication Data

Names: Murphy, Frank, 1966- author.
Title: Stand up for respect / written by Frank Murphy.
Description: Ann Arbor : Cherry Lake Publishing, 2019. | Series: Growing character | Includes index.
Identifiers: LCCN 2019007379| ISBN 9781534147447 (hardcover) | ISBN 9781534148871 (pdf) | ISBN 9781534150300 (pbk.) | ISBN 9781534151734 (hosted ebook)
Subjects: LCSH: Respect for persons–Juvenile literature. | Respect–Juvenile literature.
Classification: LCC BJ1533.R42 M87 2019 | DDC 179/.9–dc23
LC record available at https://lccn.loc.gov/2019007379

Cherry Lake Publishing would like to acknowledge the work of The Partnership for 21st Century Skills.
Please visit *www.p21.org* for more information.

Printed in the United States of America
Corporate Graphics

CONTENTS

Not looking at a person talking to you is disrespectful.

What Is Respect?

Jake and Jordan joined a new basketball team. On the first day of practice, the coach gathered all the players around him to talk about the team and some rules. Jake and Jordan noticed one teammate who wasn't looking at the coach. This person was **slouching**, with his arms folded, and he was whispering to another teammate during the coach's talk.

Talking when someone else is talking does not show respect. Listening to people

Teachers work hard to plan lessons to help you learn. Show respect by listening to what they say.

who are speaking shows respect. It shows that you respect what others have to say. It also shows that you care about your learning, which is an important way to respect yourself.

Respect is treating others the way you would want to be treated. Making fun of someone or insulting them does not show respect. A respectful person cares about other people's feelings.

Think!

Remember a time when you heard someone talking during a lesson. Did it take your attention away from what your teacher was saying? Have you ever talked during a teacher's lesson?

Trying to help people on your team is respectful.

Later, Jake and Jordan talked over ways they could help the boy be a better teammate.

They did not make a **judgment** about the boy. They were respectful of him. They both knew that they wouldn't like it if one of their teammates spoke poorly about them.

There are two things you can do when talking about someone:

1. **Think before you speak**. Try waiting a few moments before speaking about someone. Maybe even count to 10 in your mind.

2. **Be positive**. Use language that is kind and helpful. Being **negative** is not respectful.

Keeping your room clean shows respect for your parents, your things, and yourself!

Showing Respect

Showing respect at home with your family is important. Your parents might have rules about cleaning up after yourself, keeping your room clean, and going to bed at a certain

Create!

Make a list of people you respect and look up to. It might include parents, teachers, or other people who have helped you. Share the list with your parents or an adult you trust. Talk about why you respect the people on the list.

Arguing with your parents because you don't want to help around the house is disrespectful.

time. Following these rules shows respect. Showing respect at home is great practice for doing it everywhere else—at school, church or temple, people's homes, and other places. Talking back to your parents or not following rules is disrespectful.

You should respect the beliefs and lifestyles of people from all around the world.

Respecting Your World

Treating all people with respect is important. When you meet people who look, sound, or act differently than you, do not judge them. Politely ask them to tell you about themselves. Try to learn about their **culture** and their family. Learning other people's stories is a great way to show respect for someone. It shows you care and are interested in them.

It is respectful to ask to borrow something, instead of just taking it.

You can also show respect by not taking things that do not belong to you. Taking a pencil or papers from a classmate's desk without asking does not show respect. It is important to think about how you might feel if someone took your things without asking you. And, of course, damaging people's belongings, like someone's bike or a neighbor's garden, is not respectful.

Recycling helps show respect for our world.

Respecting the **environment** is another important positive action. Not littering, not wasting water, and turning off the lights when you leave a room are all simple ways to show respect for our world.

When you choose to help keep our world a healthy place, you are respecting people everywhere. And you are showing respect for people in the future!

When you give respect, you get respect.

Respect starts with you!

The respect you show for others and for all things will tell people a lot about the kind of person you are. It will also tell them how you want them to treat you.

Look!

Notice the people around you. Notice how your teachers talk to one another. Do they show respect? How could they be more respectful? Talk about your thoughts with your parents and friends.

GLOSSARY

culture (KUHL-chur) the ideas, habits, and practices of different groups of people

environment (en-VYE-ruhn-muhnt) the world around you, including the land, sea, and air

judgment (JUHJ-muhnt) an opinion or a conclusion about someone or something

negative (NEG-uh-tiv) showing only the bad side of someone or something

slouching (SLOUCH-ing) sitting, standing, or walking with your head and shoulders drooping or bent forward

FIND OUT MORE

BOOKS

Kroll, Virginia L. *Ryan Respects*. Morton Grove, IL: Albert Whitman & Company, 2006.

Roberts, Justin. *The Smallest Girl in the Smallest Grade*. New York, NY: G. P. Putnam's Sons Books for Young Readers, 2014.

Suen, Anastasia. *Show Some Respect*. Edina, MN: Magic Wagon, 2008.

WEBSITES

Kids' Health—Respect: A Way of Life

www.cyh.sa.gov.au/HealthTopics/HealthTopicDetailsKids.aspx?p=335&np=287&id=2356
Read more about respecting yourself and others.

Stories to Grow By

www.storiestogrowby.com/choose.php
Find folktales and fairy tales about respect and other good character traits.

INDEX

ABOUT THE AUTHOR

Frank Murphy has written several books for young readers. They are about famous people, historical events, and leadership. He was born in California but now lives in Pennsylvania with his family.